Are you there, Bear?

Ron Maris

GREENWILLOW BOOKS, New York

For Ellen Maris

Copyright © 1984 by Ron Maris
First published in Great Britain 1984
by Julia MacRae Books
All rights reserved. No part of this book
may be reproduced or utilized in any form
or by any means, electronic or mechanical,
including photocopying, recording or by
any information storage and retrieval
system, without permission in writing
from the Publisher, Greenwillow Books,
a division of William Morrow & Company, Inc.,
105 Madison Avenue, New York, N.Y. 10016.
Printed in Belgium
First American Edition
10 9 8 7 6 5 4 3 2 1
Library of Congress Cataloging in Publication Data
Maris, Ron.
Are you there, bear?
Summary: In a darkened bedroom, several toys
search for a bear, finally finding him reading
a book behind a chair.
[1. Toys—Fiction.   2. Teddy bears—Fiction]
I. Title.
PZ8.9.M34Ar 1984   [E]   84-4180
ISBN 0-688-03997-9
ISBN 0-688-03998-7 (lib. bdg.)

My room is dark and quiet.
Are you there, Bear?

Under my bed?

That's not a bear.
Come out, Donkey!

In my cupboard?

That's not a bear.
Come out,
Little Doll!

Up here, in my box?

That's not a bear.
Go back, Jack!

Over here, in my basket?

That's not a bear.
Come out, Raggety!

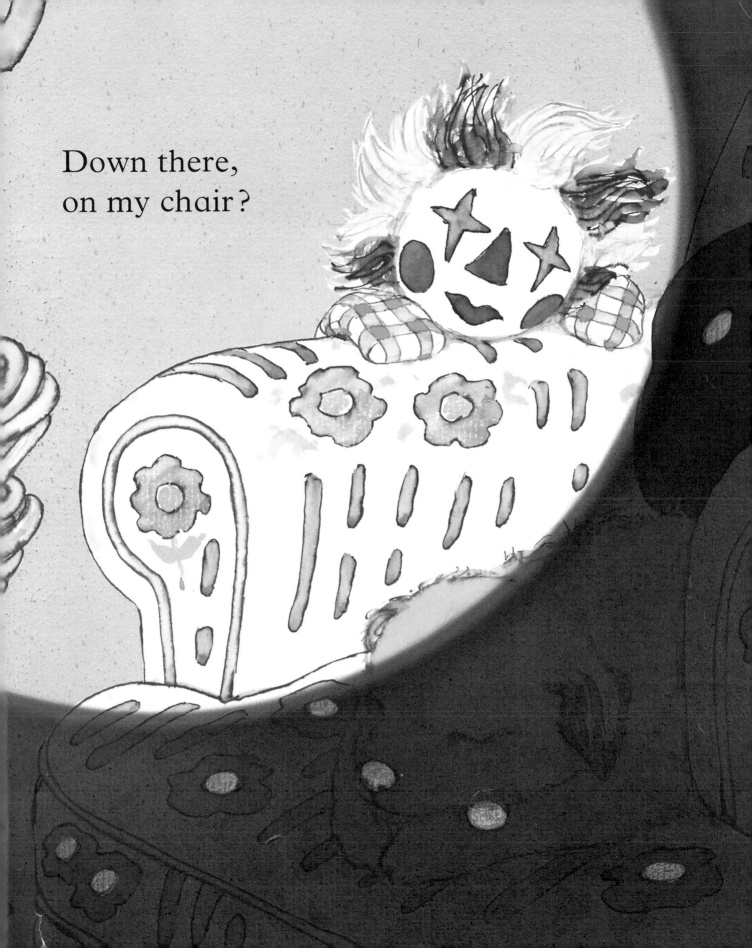

Down there,
on my chair?

That's not a bear.
Come out, Spike!

What is that?

Who is there, beside my chair?

Bear is there! With a book . . .

. . . tell us a story, Bear.